Norman's Loose Tooth

written and photographed
by
Mia Coulton

Danny and Norman were on the deck.

Norman was chewing his big, blue ball.

"Ouch!" said Norman.

"What just came out of my mouth?" asked Norman.

"It's a puppy tooth!"
said Danny.
"Put it under your pillow.
When you go to sleep,
the tooth fairy will take
the puppy tooth and leave
a surprise for you."

9

"What does the tooth fairy look like?"

wondered Norman.